E
Cu

$9.96

Curious George goes
to a toy store

DATE DUE

FE 20'91	DE 26'91	OC 2 2'92	v 2 9'93
AP 6'91	JA 2'92	NO 2 3'92	
AP 26'91	FE 7'92	JA 21'93	NV 2 9'93
MY 15'91	MR 12'92	JA 28'93	AG 1 9'93
	AP 1'92	FE 8'93	SE 15'93
JY 2'91	AP 22'92	AP 7'93	OC 11'93
AG 17'91	JE 2'92	AP 16'93	OC 23'93
AG 29'91	JY 2'92	AP 23'92	FE 7'94
SE 23'9	JY 8'92	JE 7'93	MAR 21 '94
OC 10'91	JUL 23'92	JY 1'93	MAY 20 '94
NO 4'91	SE 4'92	JY 8'93	JUN 18 '94
NO 29'91	SE 25'9		JUL 22 '94
			SEP 06 '94
			SEP 29 '94

DEMCO

Curious George®

GOES TO A TOY STORE

Adapted from the Curious George film series
Edited by Margret Rey and Alan J. Shalleck

1 9 9 0
Houghton Mifflin Company, Boston

Library of Congress Cataloging-in-Publication Data

Curious George goes to a toystore / edited by Margret Rey and
   Alan J. Shalleck.
     p. cm.
   "Adapted from the Curious George film series."
   Summary: During his visit to a new toystore, Curious George
demonstrates that monkey business can be good for business.
   ISBN 0-395-55724-0
   [1. Monkeys—Fiction. 2. Toys—Fiction. 3. Stores, Retail—Fiction.]
I. Rey, Margret. II. Shalleck, Alan J. III. Curious George goes to a
toystore (Motion picture) V. Title: Curious George goes to a toy store.
PZ7.C921645   1990   90-33509
[E]—dc20   CIP
                 AC

Printed in the United States of America

RNF ISBN 0-395-55724-0
PAP ISBN 0-395-55714-3

WOZ 10 9 8 7 6 5 4 3 2 1

"There's a new toy store opening today,
George," said his friend.
"Let's go downtown and see it."

When they arrived they saw a big crowd
waiting outside.

"I'm going to park the car," said the man
with the yellow hat. "Wait here
and don't get into trouble, George."

George ran to the front of the line.

He ran right past the surprised owner,
who had just opened the door.

There was so much to see inside . . .
dolls, bicycles, and games.

George tried to pull down a **hoop**
to play with. He pulled and pulled.

The whole pile came tumbling down.
Hoops rolled everywhere.

George picked one up and tried to Hula Hoop.

Everyone laughed and pointed at him.

Then George pretended to be a wheel.
He rolled and rolled –

13

– right into the owner!

"You're making a mess of my new store!"
the owner shouted, and tried to grab George.

George jumped up to the highest shelf to get
away. "Hey, look up there!"
shouted a little boy. "It's George."

"Mom, can he get me that doll with the pink dress that you couldn't reach?" asked a girl.

George picked up the doll
and tossed it to the girl.

"Can you reach that game for me, George?"
asked another boy.

George reached up, grabbed the game,
and threw it to the boy.

"Thanks a lot, George," he said.

"Mom, can I get that puppet over there?"
asked a girl.

How good that George was a monkey!
He jumped off the shelf, hung onto a light,
and got the puppet for the girl.

The kids laughed and cheered!
"Great show, George!" they shouted.

"What's going on here?" asked the owner.
He was angry.

"It's George!" said a boy.
"Having him work for you is a great idea."

The owner looked up.
"Well, I guess it is a good idea," he said.

George's friend came over to see what was
going on. "It's time to go now, George.
That's enough monkey business for one day."

"But monkey business is the best business,"
said the owner.

George came down from the shelf.

"Thank you, George, for making my grand
opening such a success," said the
owner. "And here's a surprise for you."

George and his friend waved good-bye
and headed for home.